SEASON TO SEASON

A Year in the CITY

by Christina Mia Gardeski

PEBBLE
a capstone imprint

Pebble Plus is published by Pebble, an imprint of Capstone.
1710 Roe Crest Drive, North Mankato, Minnesota 56003
www.capstonepub.com

Library of Congress Cataloging-in-Publication Data is available on the Library of Congress website.
ISBN 978-1-9771-1287-3 (hardcover)
ISBN 978-1-9771-2004-5 (paperback)
ISBN 978-1-9771-1288-0 (eBook PDF)

Summary: From snow plows to rooftop gardens, life in the city changes from season to season. Discover some animals that live in the city. Learn how children cool off in summer. Real-life photographs follow the seasons and capture the beauty of a year in the city.

Editorial Credits
Elyse White, designer; Jo Miller, media researcher; Tori Abraham, production specialist

Image Credits
Shutterstock: Allen.G, 5, Dmitry Burlakov, Cover, (top left), DW labs Incorporated, 7, f11photo, Cover, (bottom right), Jeff Whyte, Cover, (top right), 3, Maksymenko Nataliia, 11, MarynaG, 19, place-to-be, 9, Ryan DeBerardinis, 17, 21, Sean Pavone, 13, Songquan Deng, Cover, (bottom left), Wong Ze Ying, 15

Design Elements
Shutterstock: Alexander Ryabintsev, Minohek

Printed and bound in China.
002493

Note to Parents and Teachers

The Season to Season set supports national science standards related to earth science. This book describes and illustrates how life in a city changes with the seasons throughout the year. The images support early readers in understanding the text. The repetition of words and phrases helps early readers learn new words. This book also introduces early readers to subject-specific vocabulary words, which are defined in the Glossary section. Early readers may need assistance to read some words and to use the Table of Contents, Glossary, Read More, Internet Sites, Critical Thinking Questions, and Index sections of the book.

All internet sites appearing in back matter were available and accurate when this book was sent to press.

Table of Contents

Spring Is Here!

Water flows from the fountain. A new season begins. Spring is here! Cherry blossoms cover the park. Dogs on leashes walk past crowds.

The farmers market opens.
Visitors come from around the
world. Animal babies are born.
Hawks soar overhead.

Hello, Summer!

The seasons change. Days get longer. The air is hot. Hello, summer! Rooftop gardens pop with flowers and vegetables.

People picnic in the park or eat at sidewalk tables. Squirrels and pigeons are always close by. Children cool off in pools or sprinklers.

Fall Appears!

Soon days grow cooler. Fall appears! The leaves change color. The farmers market closes for winter. Cafes move their tables back inside.

Squirrels check benches for scraps. Pigeons nest in bridges and parking garages. They do not fly away in winter. Other animals begin to hibernate.

Welcome, Winter!

Snow falls on the city.

The seasons change again.

Welcome, winter! Plows make

piles of snow. People shovel

sidewalks. Icicles hang above.

The city stays busy day and
night. Skaters fill the ice rink.
Visitors bundle up to walk
to museums and shows.
Lights twinkle everywhere.

Soon spring will warm the city. The seasons change four times each year. But one thing stays the same. Life in the city keeps moving!

Glossary

cafe—a restaurant that is usually small in size and has less food on the menu than a big restaurant

farmers market—a shopping area where farmers sell fresh fruits and vegetables or homemade goods

hibernate—to rest during the winter; when animals hibernate their body temperature drops and breathing slows

icicle—a long, hanging piece of ice that forms when water drips and freezes

museum—a building that collects and displays historic, rare, or valuable objects like artwork and fossils

parking garage—a large garage where many cars or trucks can park

pigeon—a plump bird with short legs that lives in cities throughout the world

season—one of the four parts of the year: winter, spring, summer, and fall are seasons

Read More

Carney, Elizabeth. *Animals in the City*. New York: National Geographic Children's Books, 2019.

Lynch, Annabelle. *Seasons*. New York: Windmill Books, 2016.

Spilsbury, Louise and Richard. *A Nature Walk in the City*. Chicago: Heinemann Library, 2015.

Internet Sites

Bronx Zoo: Meet the Stars of the Children's Zoo
https://bronxzoo.com/updates/stars-of-childrens-zoo

PBS Learning Media: About the Seasons
https://nj.pbslearningmedia.org/resource/evscps.sci.life.boutseas/about-the-seasons/

Critical Thinking Questions

1. If you lived in the city what sounds would you hear in winter that you would not hear in summer?

2. Where might animals live in big cities? Why?

3. How is spring in the city different from spring on a farm? How is it the same?

Index